Bantam Books in the Choose Your Own Adventure® Series
Ask your bookseller for the books you have missed

THE ANTIMATTER FORMULA

BY JAY LEIBOLD

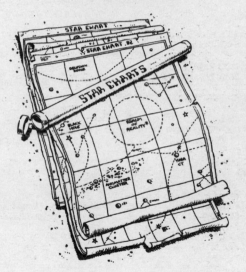

ILLUSTRATED BY FRANK BOLLE

An R. A. Montgomery Book

BANTAM BOOKS
TORONTO · NEW YORK · LONDON · SYDNEY · AUCKLAND

RL 4, IL age 10 and up

THE ANTIMATTER FORMULA
A Bantam Book / June 1986

CHOOSE YOUR OWN ADVENTURE ® *is a registered trademark of Bantam Books, Inc. Registered in U.S. Patent and Trademark Office and elsewhere.*

Original conception of Edward Packard

ISBN 0-553-25741-2

Published simultaneously in the United States and Canada

Bantam Books are published by Bantam Books, Inc. Its trademark, consisting of the words "Bantam Books" and the portrayal of a rooster, is Registered in U.S. Patent and Trademark Office and in other countries. Marca Registrada. Bantam Books, Inc., 666 Fifth Avenue, New York, New York 10103.

PRINTED IN THE UNITED STATES OF AMERICA

O   0 9 8 7 6 5 4 3 2 1

THE ANTIMATTER FORMULA

WARNING!!!

Do not read this book straight through from beginning to end! These pages contain many different adventures you can have as you try to unravel the mystery of the strange world in which you wake up. As you read along you will be able to make choices. Your choices will determine whether or not you succeed in solving the mystery.

Many unusual people, creatures, and worlds may help or hinder you in your quest. You are responsible for your fate because *you* make the decisions. After you make a choice, follow the instructions to find out what happens next.

Be careful! It will take ingenuity and resourcefulness to resolve your dilemma.

Good luck!

SPECIAL WARNING!!!

In the course of your adventures you may come into contact with parallel worlds. There are many worlds in the universe—perhaps an infinite number. Parallel worlds exist side by side, but are sealed off from one another. Each is woven of its own unique fabric of space and time. Some worlds have had an evolution and history very much like our own, and may seem just like ours; others have evolved very differently, and may be home to all kinds of odd creatures and ideas.

You wake up one morning and sense that something is wrong. An odd quiet has settled on the house. You sit up. Everything in your room looks the same as usual. Still, you can't shake the feeling that you've woken up in a different place, as if you've been traveling and for a moment can't remember where you are.

You get up and look out your window—the street is empty, but that's not unusual. You get dressed and brush your hair in the mirror. You look the same as always.

Your footsteps seem unnaturally loud in the hallway and on the stairs. It makes you feel as if it's early on Sunday morning—except you know it is a Wednesday morning in June, in Berkeley, California. You are on summer vacation, and today is your day off from your summer job. Your parents, who are physicists at the university lab, have probably already left for work.

You stop for a moment at the bottom of the stairs. The only sound is the ticking of the living room clock, keeping the beat of the silence. It's the first time, you think, you've *ever heard* silence.

Turn to page 4.

You dial your parents' number at the lab, but they don't answer. No one does. You put down the phone and tell yourself there must be a simple explanation for this.

You know that your parents are involved in antimatter research, and you've wondered what they meant when they talked about the delicate boundaries between parallel worlds. It sounded as if they thought they could use antimatter to travel between parallel worlds. But when you asked questions, they said they couldn't tell you any more about it. They had not even told the university or the government about it. Wondering if their research is connected with the strange emptiness around you, you decide to go to the lab.

You get your bike and ride through the deserted streets. When you reach the lab, everything looks normal—cars in the parking lot, bicycles in the rack, trees, grass. But there are no people.

Go on to the next page.

The main door is unlocked, and inside, the lights are on. You walk through the empty halls and up the staircase to the third floor. The door to your parents' lab is open. As usual, equipment is spread all over the counters and on the floor. But in one corner of the lab, you notice that some of the equipment has been knocked over, as if there was a struggle. And sitting on the counter is something you've never seen there before—a television. It is one of the new, small, wafer-thin types. You think it must be connected to your parents' research.

Suddenly you freeze. There are footsteps in the hall. You listen for a moment. The footsteps are coming closer.

If you wait and see who it is, turn to page 9.

If you decide to take the TV and hide in a closet, turn to page 38.

Telling yourself your imagination is getting out of hand, you sit down to eat breakfast. Everything is set out as usual on the kitchen table.

After breakfast you go outside and walk down the block. You see no one. You walk up to Telegraph Avenue, which is usually busy with morning traffic. It is empty. You call out, "Hello!" The sound of your voice startles you. A few birds sing in the trees, but there are no human sounds.

You go back to the house and try to control your feeling of panic. The ticking of the living room clock becomes oppressive.

You go out to the garage. The car is still there, but your parents' bikes are gone. They must have taken them to the lab, you tell yourself.

Looking at the car, you get an idea—if no one is around, maybe you should take it out and explore the city. Your uncle taught you how to drive on his farm, so you think you can handle a car. It might be a good time to take it for a drive.

On the other hand, maybe you should call your parents at the lab.

If you decide to take the car out for a drive, turn to page 108.

If you call your parents at the lab, turn to page 2.

Fingley sighs. "Your parents are involved in antimatter research. They came up with a device that can disrupt the boundaries between parallel worlds."

"What are parallel worlds?" you ask.

"It's very complicated," Fingley says, sounding a little impatient. "Some people believe that the universe is composed of many separate but parallel worlds. The antimatter device can rupture the boundaries of space and time that keep the worlds separate—causing anyone near the device to be transported to another world."

He pauses and shakes his head sadly. "They wouldn't share their research with anyone—they said it was too dangerous. But the FBI got wind of it and started to snoop around. I tried to get your parents to confide in me . . ." He shrugs. "Now look what's happened."

"Where is everybody?" you ask.

"The fact is, due to, ah, an accident, I have been transported to a parallel world almost exactly like Earth. Somehow you came along with me."

Go on to the next page.

You let that sink in, then gesture toward the TV behind you. "Is that the antimatter device?"

"Yes," Fingley says. "I must take it apart. It's our only hope of returning to our world and putting things back to normal."

You look at the TV. "Does it work like a regular TV?"

"In a manner of speaking. After you turn it on, you can switch between worlds by changing the channel. But beyond that, I don't know how it works. That's why I must take it apart. Now please stand aside."

If you let him take the TV, turn to page 11.

If you think you should keep it away from him, turn to page 97.

You watch the door as the footsteps approach.

"Dr. Fingley!" you exclaim.

The man entering the doorway halts abruptly. At first he looks shocked, then he recognizes you. Ronald Fingley is a colleague of your parents whom you've met once or twice.

"Fancy meeting you here," he says, eyeing the TV behind you.

"Yes. I can't figure out what's going on. Where is everybody?"

"It seems there's been, ah, a little mistake," Fingley replies, coming into the lab.

"What kind of mistake?" you ask.

"Well, it's rather hard to explain, because I haven't figured out all the details." As he talks, Fingley moves toward the counter behind you. You wonder what he wants. "You see," he continues, "your parents are involved in some rather controversial research . . ."

You realize he is edging toward the TV, but you don't know why. You move between him and the television set.

"Go on," you say.

Turn to page 6.

You land on a deserted planet, leave the transporter, and sit down in an empty space. You close your eyes and begin to meditate on the planet earth. Going without food or water (which you don't have anyway) for days and then weeks, you concentrate on the planet and your life there. You imagine all the little details of it; you unlock all your memories.

Several times you feel it coming closer and closer; you can almost reach out and touch it. Each time that happens, you get ready to open your eyes, but then the sensation recedes from you.

Finally, after you've lost track of how long you've been sitting, you feel that Earth is really there, all around you. You can hear it, smell it, taste it. You wait a moment to make sure. Then, you open your eyes and—

The End

You hand the TV to Dr. Fingley.

"You've done the right thing," he says, patting you on the head, which makes you wish you hadn't given it to him. "Now you run along." He leaves the lab and walks down the hall.

"Wait a minute," you say, running to catch up. "I thought you were going to get us back to the regular world."

"Indeed I will," he replies, "just as soon as I figure out how this machine works. It's too bad your parents were too selfish to tell me its working principle." Fingley pauses at the entrance to his lab. He smiles as he closes the door in your face. "Don't worry, it won't take me long. And when we do return, I shall be hailed as a genius."

But the months pass and Fingley fails to crack the secret of the antimatter device. He takes it apart and can't figure out how to put it back together. You doubt he ever will.

Meanwhile, you find that life is lonely with no one else around. Well, you think, perhaps if you begin studying physics, some day you will come up with a way to get back to the world you know. But for now, you're stuck in this empty parallel world with Dr. Fingley as your only companion.

The End

At an intersection you brake and make a sharp left into the park. Fingley speeds on past you, but then he slows and turns left. He jumps the curb and drives across the grass to cut you off as you race down a bike path.

You change direction and pedal hard toward a grove of trees. You manage to reach the trees before Fingley does, but he pulls onto the bike path, which is just wide enough for his car, and accelerates. His car pulls closer and closer to you. In a few seconds he will run into you and knock you off your bike.

Ahead on your right, another path turns sharply downhill and winds through a rock garden. Coming up on your left is a lake with some pedal boats moored to a dock.

take the path to the right through the rock garden, turn to page 21.

ou go for the dock, turn to page 58.

A crowd of people is waiting on the deck of the ocean liner when you land. "Where's the device?" the FBI men demand. Sheepishly you explain what happened. After they give you a good chewing out, they rush off to try to catch the Russian boat.

The liner pulls into San Francisco the next morning and you call your parents to come get you. They listen patiently as you tell your story, but they can't hide their horror at the outcome.

"This is terrible," your father says. "Now there will almost certainly be an antimatter arms race and the government will make life very difficult for us if we don't help them in it."

You have an idea. "Maybe," you suggest, "you could build a new antimatter device before the government clamps down. Then we could escape to another world."

"It might be possible," your father says. "We've got all the materials at the lab . . ."

Your parents set to work secretly in the basement of your house, and within a week they have a new antimatter device. "It's crude," says your father, "but it should work."

That night, after saying good-bye to your closest friends, you and your parents gather in the living room. When you are ready, you lean over and turn the channel. . . .

The End

Just as Fingley springs, you run out the door with the TV.

"I must have that device!" Fingley cries.

You dash through the hall, down the steps, and out the door. Fingley's shoes clatter on the floor as he pursues you. You put the TV in your bike basket, leap on your bicycle, and ride away.

Fingley runs to his car, starts it up, and pulls out of the parking lot with a screech. Soon he is on your tail.

You turn on to Telegraph Avenue and pedal faster. But Fingley is gaining on you. You stop, carry your bike over the divider, and set off in the opposite direction. Looking back, you see Fingley put on the brakes, skid in a half-circle, and come back after you. Although he is still on the other side of the divider, he is catching up. He pulls even, and you realize you're not going to be able to escape him, at least not on your bike on the city streets.

Coming up on your left is a park. You could turn in and try to elude Fingley on the bike paths. Or you could hop off your bike, run by the houses on your right, and hope to lose him in the maze of backyards.

If you decide to cut into the park, turn to page 12.

If you decide to escape to the ho turn to p

You grab a vine and pause to look into the gorge before you swing across. It's a long way down.

The sound of the Oglemorooth close behind gets you moving. You grip the vine, take a run, and swing out over the gorge. About halfway across, the vine breaks and you plunge, screaming, into the depths.

The End

es,
ge 19.

18

You make a dive for Fingley, but you miss! He leaps over you and grabs the TV.

Fingley runs out of the lab, and you chase him down the hall. He has a head start, but you are faster. You make a flying tackle in the hallway. He crashes to the ground and the TV skids away from him.

You scramble over to it. On the bottom of it you notice a button that is labeled RESET. In a flash you realize what it must be for. You switch the TV on, then start to push the RESET button.

"Wait!" Fingley says. "Don't press that button."

"Why not?" you say. "It might take things back to where they started from."

"No!" he cries. "It will ruin everything! You must give me the TV. It's our only hope!"

You put your finger on the RESET button.

"Please," Fingley pleads. "You must not do this. You must not take us back to the regular world. This is my one chance to discover the secret of the antimatter device—"

Turn to page 24.

You make a sharp turn into a driveway, hop off your bike, and, carrying the TV, jump over a gate into a backyard. There you check for escape routes. But you see no quick way out of the yard, so you go into the house, hoping to find a good place to hole up until Fingley goes away.

In a back bedroom you find an old wardrobe full . of clothes. You wedge yourself in behind the clothes, pull the doors shut, and settle down to wait. You decide you should stay in there for at least an hour to be sure Fingley has gone away.

A few minutes later you hear a car pull up outside the house. The engine is shut off and the car door opens and closes. You hear footsteps, then the front door to the house opens. You begin to sweat. You can hear Fingley methodically searching each of the rooms. It may be only a matter of time before he finds you. You put your fingers on the channel switch.

Fingley enters the room. You hear him shuffling around, looking for you. Then the wardrobe doors are flung open and the clothes are pulled aside.

"Aha!" Fingley cries. At that moment you switch the TV on and change the channel.

Turn to page 26.

You stop and turn to face the FBI agents. When they catch up with you, you calmly hand over the TV, explaining that you were just trying to keep it away from Dr. Fingley.

The shorter agent says, "You've done a good job. There may even be a medal in store for you. Now we'll take you back to shore with us."

You've been curious all this time to know where you are—and now you find out that you're on an ocean liner! It's not far from shore, though, and the FBI men take you to the dock in their launch.

You call your parents and they come to pick you up. They are relieved to see you, but they look unhappy when you tell them the antimatter device is in the hands of the FBI.

"Well, I guess we're glad to find out that it actually works," your father says. "We hadn't tested it before Dr. Fingley took it."

"You see," your mother says, "we didn't want to reveal the device because we were afraid the government might put it to destructive uses. I guess we can only hope it doesn't."

The End

You zoom down the path, but must put on your brakes to handle the curves through the rock garden.

Looking back, you can hardly believe Fingley is following you, but he is. His car is bouncing over rocks and plants as it comes down the path.

You look ahead again. All of a sudden you realize you've missed a curve. A park bench is right in front of you, and there is no way to avoid it. At the last minute you grab the TV. Your bike strikes the bench and you go flying over it.

Turn to page 37.

You manage to figure out the navigation system of the transporter and land safely on Yuba CT. As you leave the transporter, you are greeted by a cheering throng of khaki-clad people. Someone explains to you that you are a hero on this rebel planet because you captured an Imperial transporter. You receive an award and many congratulations.

When the excitement is over, you find a scientist in a tent in the main encampment of Yuba CT. You tell him you want to know how to get to planet Earth.

"Planet Earth?" the scientist says. "There is no hard evidence that it actually exists. But most speculations place it in the Realm of Unreality."

"Can I look for it?" you ask.

"Oh, no, I wouldn't recommend it," he says. "No one who has ventured in has ever returned from the Realm of Unreality. Only the Empire has the technology to go into that area. I'd say your best bet would be to join us in our fight to overthrow the Empire. If we succeed, we can get our hands on their technology and then we'll be able to find a way to Earth."

You resign yourself to a long wait before attempting a return to Earth. At least it looks as if your life will be exciting in the meantime.

The End

You press the button. Suddenly the hallway is crowded with people. Some of them are scientists who recognize you and run to get your parents.

"You're back! Good work!" your mother says when she arrives. She turns to Fingley. "You should be ashamed of yourself!" she scolds.

"He stole the antimatter device from us and activated it," your father explains. "That's how all this got started. If you hadn't gotten it back for us, who knows what havoc he might have wreaked with the universe!"

The End

After slipping into the cabin and quickly exchanging the TV, you go back down the corridor. You open the door to the deck. Coming toward you are the two FBI agents.

"Hand it over," the shorter one says.

You sigh and turn over the TV. "I guess I have no choice."

"Don't worry," the taller one says. "We'll see that it gets into the proper hands."

The agents depart immediately in their launch. You return to the cabin where you left the antimatter device. It is still there. You take it and manage to find a box in which to conceal it.

Your plan works brilliantly. The ocean liner pulls into San Francisco the next morning. You call your parents from the waterfront, and tell them you have a surprise for them—if they come pick you up.

The End

You find that you are standing in a room full of men in black tie and women in evening gowns. Everyone's holding champagne glasses. The room seems to be rising and falling. You are holding the TV, facing Dr. Fingley. Both of you look around in surprise.

"Are we back in the regular world?" you ask.

"I guess so," Fingley says. He eyes the TV. But you are not worried about Fingley. You see two men, one tall, one short, approaching Fingley from behind. As the taller one grabs Fingley's arm, you slip into the crowd, staying close enough to hear the man say to Fingley, "Okay, Doctor, we've finally caught up with you. Where's the device?"

"I—I don't know what you're talking about," Fingley stammers.

"You can't fool us," the shorter man says menacingly. "We're the FBI. We know you stole it from the lab."

"Yes," Fingley says, "but I don't have it. I know who does, though."

You don't need to hear any more. They're going to be after you very soon. You thread your way through the crowd. There's a commotion behind you—someone is telling you to stop. You look for a door, but then it occurs to you that maybe you *should* give the TV to the agents.

If you decide to give the TV to the FBI men, turn to page 20.

If you make a fast exit, turn to page 35.

Perhaps the best thing after all would be to call your parents and ask them what to do—if you can get to the communications room, that is.

Just then the door at the other end of the corridor opens. A man with a friendly red face sticks his head out and says, "Psst! I can help you escape!"

If you accept the man's help, turn to page 30.

If you want to try to call your parents instead, turn to page 32.

You pedal furiously to make Fingley think you're trying to escape as he approaches in the motorboat. He revs up the engine and increases his speed. When he is nearly upon you, you suddenly turn the boat around and ram him.

The collision splinters the boats and sends both of you flying. You have the TV, which you try to keep above the water as you grip the edge of the pedal boat. Fingley flounders in the water a few yards away from you.

"Help!" he cries. "I can't swim!"

"What can I do?" you call back to him. "I'll have to let go of the antimatter device to come save you."

"The RESET button," he cries desperately. "Turn the TV on and push the RESET button! It's on the bottom of the TV."

You switch the TV on, then quickly press the RESET button. Suddenly you are no longer in the water. You are lying dripping wet on the floor of your living room. Your parents are standing over you.

"You're back!" your mother exclaims. "And you've rescued the antimatter device!" Then she turns to Fingley, who is gasping on the carpet on the other side of the room. "As for you, Dr. Fingley, you are in a lot of trouble."

Fingley glares at you. Still, he has to be grateful to you for saving his life.

The End

Cautiously you approach the man at the end of the corridor. "Who are you?"

"Let's just say I'm a friend," he says with a smile.

"How can we escape them?" you ask. "Sooner or later they will search the whole ship. They have us trapped."

"You're right, of course," he says. "That's why we must leave the ship. Now come."

You follow the man. He takes you through a labyrinth of little passages to a storage room. Stowed behind some crates are two large suitcases. The man hauls them out and opens them up. Inside each suitcase is a jet pack!

He straps one on, then helps you with the other. After he shows you how the hand controls work, he picks up the TV and says, "You'd better let me carry this. You'll need both hands, since you're a beginner."

Reluctantly you agree with him and follow him through a door to a narrow outdoor passageway.

"Ready?" the man asks. You nod.

Turn to page 41.

You can't bear the thought of being tricked and not doing anything about it.

You turn as if to head back for the ship, but then make a large circle around to the other side of the KGB man, staying behind him. You pick up speed and swoop in like a hawk. He is taken completely by surprise when you crash down on him. He loses his grip on the TV, and you grab it in both arms. But the collision has disabled your jet pack. You are falling to the water.

You have only one hope. You grope desperately for the dials on the TV. You turn the TV on and switch the channel.

Turn to page 93.

32

"No thanks!" you call to the man at the end of the corridor. You run back the way you came, dash through a door, and climb another flight of steps to another deck.

You manage to find the communications room and get the operator to put through an emergency call to your parents. Quickly you explain your situation to them. They do not seem very surprised.

"We were afraid the government might be after it," your father says. "We think they want to develop it into some kind of weapon. That's why we didn't tell them about it."

"Then I shouldn't give it to them?" you ask.

"It's a lot to ask," your father says, "but if you can possibly help it—just don't put yourself in any danger. Don't—"

"I hear them coming now," you cut in. "I'd better go. Don't worry."

Turn to page 39.

"Let's take back the fake spoon," you say. "It'll save us a lot of trouble."

Sandina just shrugs, so the three of you turn back, cross the pass, and return to the well. Sandina lowers you in the bucket. Her last words are, "For your sake, I hope it works."

The orange spider seems very pleased to receive the spoon. As he crawls back up his thread, he tells you to ring a doorbell set in the stone door, and that the man inside is named Malgernopf.

The ruse seems to be working so far. You ring the doorbell, and the door swings open. Malgernopf glares at you. "Well? What do you want?"

"I want the TV back," you say.

Malgernopf curls his lip and laughs. "Ha ha! Don't you think I saw you dig up the fake spoon on TV? I despise fakes! You made me so angry, I threw the TV out the window. Now leave me alone!"

Once again the door slams in your face. You and Luther look at each other unhappily. It appears you are stuck here, with no one left to help you.

The End

You locate a door and push your way toward it. The agents spot you and rush after you, but you push two of the champagne sippers into them, which causes general confusion.

You run through the door and down a hallway. Another door leads you outside, onto some kind of deck. The floor still seems to be swaying. It's night, and you feel the wind on your face. You go to a metal railing at the edge of the deck and look over. The sea is rushing below. You're on an ocean liner!

Wondering how you're going to escape the FBI men now, you run up a staircase to another deck. You are in a corridor with numbered doors. They look like passenger cabins.

The door to one of the cabins is open and something inside catches your eye. It is a television set that looks exactly like your antimatter device. You have an idea: What if you were to exchange the antimatter device for the TV in the cabin, hand over the duplicate TV to the agents, then come back later for the real one? The only other thing you can think of is to call your parents and ask them what to do.

If you make the exchange, turn to page 25.

If you think it's wiser not to, turn to page 27.

You find yourself looking at the screen, rather than around you, to see where you are. You are in a dark passageway, with a stone door in front of you. Suddenly the door opens, a little man with a big nose and pointed ears runs out, grabs the TV, and scampers behind the door, laughing. The door shuts with a bang that rings in your ears.

"Hey!" you say. You look at Luther. "What's going on here?" You try the door, but it won't budge.

Luther shrugs. "Beats me!"

Turn to page 52.

When you open your eyes, you are still holding the TV. Your bike is smashed against the park bench, and Fingley's car is off to one side, overturned.

You get up and find that you are bruised but able to walk. You right your bike, straighten it out as best you can, put the TV in your basket, and ride shakily down the path.

You don't get very far before you see that the park is full of people! The crash must have activated the device and returned you to the world you know—at least it looks like the normal world, only it is later in the day, almost evening.

You take the TV back to the lab and hide it in a closet. Then you get on your bike and ride home. You walk into the house and your mother exclaims, "Where have you been?"

"Just out riding my bicycle," you say.

"Your father and I have been looking all over for you! You and Dr. Fingley. They found Fingley in the middle of the park in his car, upside down. Now isn't that strange!"

The End

Moving very quietly, you grab the TV and slip into one of the storage closets against the wall. Then you hold your breath and listen.

The footsteps come closer and closer. They come into the lab. "My device!" a man's voice cries out. "Where's my device?"

The voice seems vaguely familiar, but you can't quite place it. You hear the man run out of the room and down the hall.

Cautiously you come out of the closet. You set the TV on the counter and decide to turn it on. Maybe there will be some news about what is going on.

The picture materializes after a moment. At first you don't realize what is on the screen, but then it sinks in: You are looking at yourself—in the lab looking at the TV! You jump back with a gasp. The person on TV jumps back too.

If you change the channel, turn to page 46.

If you turn off the TV, turn to page 51.

You dash out of the communications room. The agents are waiting for you at the other end of the corridor. "Stop!" they cry.

You turn the other way and run the length of the deck. At the end, you go down a stairway and along the deck below in the opposite direction. Looking back, you see only the short man. But then you see the taller agent coming at you from the other direction. The agents close in from both sides.

You consider your options. Should you throw the antimatter device into the ocean to prevent it from being put to destructive uses? Or should you escape by activating the machine, even though you may never get back to this world again?

If you pitch the TV overboard, turn to page 59.

If you decide to turn it on, turn to page 62.

You both fire up your jet packs and lift off. It's exhilarating to fly over the water. "This is great!" you call to the man who has rescued you. "Where are we going?"

He laughs in a way you don't like. "If I were you, my friend, I would go back to the ship while you still have enough fuel left. You see, your fuel tank is only a quarter full. You will never make it to the KGB boat that is waiting for me." He laughs again and holds up the TV. "Thanks for the antimatter formula!"

You are mad. You want the TV back, but you're afraid to risk plunging into the cold water when your fuel runs out.

If you return to the ocean liner, turn to page 13.

If you want to try to get the TV away from the KGB man, turn to page 31.

Your hand reaches the channel switch just as the lizard's claw is about to come down.

You find yourself on the ground, covered with dust, next to the TV. Behind you someone is clapping and yelling, "Bravo!"

You turn and see a short man with thick limbs jumping up and down and clapping. His blue eyes flash brightly as he leans down and exclaims, "Very good! Much better than when you were in the laboratory with no one else around! That was boring!"

You sit up and look at this strange man. He grabs your hand and pumps it. "My name is Luther! How do you do!"

You point to the TV and ask, "Did that bring me here?"

"Of course!" Luther says. "That's how you switch between worlds!"

"You mean—between parallel worlds?"

"Of course! What else would you use it for?"

"Well, where I come from," you explain, "we sit in our living rooms and watch TV, we don't participate in it."

"How bizarre! You just sit and watch?"

"Yes—it's, you know, entertainment."

"But how can that entertain you? How boring!"

Go on to the next page.

You think about that for a minute, then point at the TV and ask, "How does it work? How does it switch you between worlds?"

"How does it work? I don't know! We don't know how anything works! And we don't care! Now, let's go somewhere else."

You watch as Luther leans down and turns the channel.

Turn to page 36.

Quickly you scramble up a moss-laden tree and try to stay hidden on a branch that hangs out over the gorge.

The Oglemorooth comes panting after you, blindly smashing his way through the underbrush. He doesn't see you—or the gorge. He steps right over the edge, and with a terrible scream, falls to the bottom.

You pause for a moment to consider the Oglemorooth's fate. Then you come down from the tree and head back to the trail. Sandina and Luther are waiting for you behind a rock on the mountainside.

"Thank goodness you're all right!" Luther says. "We were beginning to get worried."

You tell them about the Oglemorooth's death, and the three of you hike over the pass and back to the well. Sandina congratulates you and Luther on your success, then lowers you down the well.

The orange spider is amazed when you present him with the spoon. "I didn't think it was possible!" he says. "Nevertheless, I'm very pleased. Now I suppose I should keep my half of the bargain. The little man who has your TV is called Malgernopf. You'll find a doorbell there in the stone to the right of his door."

The button is exactly where the spider says it is. You press it and wait to confront Malgernopf.

Turn to page 64.

"Very well," says Sandina. "I will take take you. But if the Oglemorooth catches you, he'll eat you."

You and Luther set off with Sandina to find the Oglemorooth. She leads you over a high, rocky mountain pass, which descends toward a deep, seemingly bottomless valley.

The three of you stop for a rest on the way down into the valley. "Four times a year," Sandina explains, "the Oglemorooth comes over this pass to gather spider eggs. He lives in a shack at the bottom of this valley. But we must wait a while before we continue. Every afternoon the Oglemorooth takes a nap, and that is the only time you have any hope of getting his spoon."

Turn to page 50.

A giant green lizard appears on the screen. It's a huge scaly thing with horrible eyes. It has cornered three tiny figures in chain mail against some rocks. The three cower behind their shields as the lizard advances on them. Spears stick out of the lizard's back like toothpicks.

You're so absorbed by this picture that you don't notice you are no longer in your parents' lab. But when the lizard opens its mouth and lets out a roar, you suddenly realize it's real. You jump to your feet and turn around. Before your eyes is the scene on TV!

On the ground beside you is a spiked ball and chain. Without thinking, you pick it up, whirl it over your head, and fling it at the lizard. The ball flies through the air and makes a direct hit on the lizard's neck. Green blood spurts out. The lizard roars in pain, rears back, and turns to face the new threat. Now it advances on you with great crashing steps, its jaws dripping.

Desperately you look around. No more weapons! You turn, trip, and fall to the ground. The lizard's breath is hot on your neck.

If you get up and run, turn to page 54.

If you scramble to the TV and try to change the channel, turn to page 42.

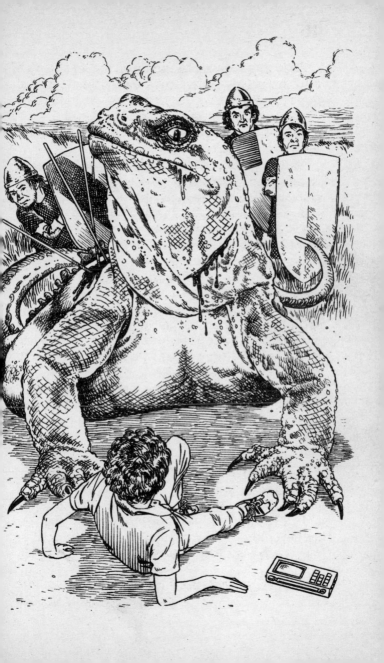

"Okay," you tell the spider. "We'll get the spoon of the Oglemorooth, if you promise to get us in that door."

"I promise," the spider says.

"Now, how do we find this Oglemorooth?" you ask.

"First you have to get out of the cavern," the spider says. "Go down the passageway behind you, take three lefts then a right. You will come to a bucket at the bottom of a well. Pull on the bucket and someone will haul you up."

Luther repeats the instructions as the spider spins back up out of sight.

You and Luther feel your way along the dark passage, taking three lefts and a right, and come to a place where a sliver of light filters into the cave. The bucket is there. You pull the rope. Far above, a bell rings.

"Who is it?" a voice calls down the well.

"The orange spider sent us," you shout back.

"Get in the bucket," the voice instructs.

After you and Luther are hauled up in the bucket, you climb out and find yourself in a green clearing beside a cottage.

"My name is Sandina," a voice says. "What is your business here?"

You turn to face a woman with long black hair and bright orange eyes. She wears a black tunic decorated with odd symbols. "We're looking for the Oglemorooth," you say. "We're supposed to bring back his spoon."

Go on to the next page.

Sandina laughs. "That spider must have put you up to this. He's always trying to get people to steal the Oglemorooth's spoon, but no one has succeeded. The Oglemorooth is a nasty creature, and he doesn't care about anything but eating. He sleeps with the spoon under his pillow. What makes you think you can get it from him?"

"We have to!" Luther says. "Or we'll be stuck in this world forever!"

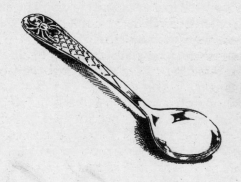

Turn to page 45.

While you are talking, Luther wanders over to a rocky outcropping. "Hey, come here!" he calls.

You and Sandina walk over to where Luther is kicking apart a mound of dirt. He extracts something from it. "It's a spoon!" he says.

Sandina takes it. "It looks just like the one the Oglemorooth uses."

"There are mounds all over the place," you say.

"It must be a kind of spoon graveyard," Sandina suggests, "where he buries all the spoons he's rejected."

"Hey," Luther says. "Why don't we just take this spoon back to the spider? He won't be able to tell the difference. Then we won't have to risk our lives with the Oglemorooth."

"I don't know," Sandina cautions. "It's true your chances of getting the real spoon aren't very good, and this might be an easy way out. But it might backfire on you."

*If you agree with Luther's plan,
turn to page 33.*

*If you decide you must get the real spoon,
turn to page 70.*

With the TV off, you sit down to think what to do. You decide the best thing might be to drive around the city and see if you can find out something that way.

You leave the lab and ride your bike back home.

Turn to page 108.

At that moment, a glowing orange spider descends from the rock above on an orange thread. The spider stops in front of your eyes and says, in a small voice, "I can tell you how to open the door."

"How?" you ask eagerly.

"First you must bring me a prize," the spider says. "You must bring me the spoon of the Oglemorooth."

"What is the Oglemorooth?" you ask Luther.

"I don't know exactly," Luther says, "but I've heard he's awful!"

"The Oglemorooth," the spider explains, "lives in a faraway valley, and with his spoon eats his favorite food—spider eggs. Once you get his spoon from him, he will no longer eat spider eggs."

"But," you object, "he can just eat them with something else."

"Oh, no," the spider says. "He's very finicky. He wouldn't use another spoon. At least not for a very long time. Now, will you carry out my request?"

*If you agree to the spider's request,
turn to page 48.*

*If you decide you have no time for it,
turn to page 66.*

The lizard lumbers after you as you run. Looking back, you see one of its giant claws crush the TV to bits.

In front of you is a dense forest. You run as hard as you can and reach the trees before the lizard gets you. It stops at the edge of the forest, unable to see where you've gone. You hide behind a log, and eventually the lizard gives up on you.

You meet the men in chain mail as you walk through the forest. They tell you they escaped while the lizard was chasing you. You expect to hear words of gratitude.

Instead, one of the men cuffs you on the ear and shouts, "What are you, some kind of fool?"

You step back in surprise. "What do you mean?"

"You let the lizard destroy the TV set, you idiot! It was our only hope of getting out of this place."

One of the others takes the man's arm and says, "Take it easy, Gondor. It couldn't be helped."

"Bah!" Gondor says and glares at you. "You could have picked it up before you ran. Now you're stuck here with the rest of us. This miserable world is ruled by lizards, and to them we're nothing but meat. Pretty soon our species will be extinct, unless we can figure out some way to get out of here."

Gondor has you put in chains, taken back to his castle, and thrown into the dungeon. "If you suffer your punishment well," he says, "we might make you a knight and let you fight the lizards. If not, we'll use you as bait."

The End

You tiptoe back to the door, where Luther and Sandina are waiting. You all go outside so you can talk. "I can't get the spoon," you whisper. "We've got to get the Oglemorooth off his pillow somehow. How about if you two make some noise outside his window? I'll hide under the cot, and when he chases after you, I'll grab the spoon."

"It sounds dangerous," Sandina says, "but we can try it. When the Oglemorooth comes after us, we'll take another path that circles back up the mountain. You take the one we came on. Run like mad when you get the spoon."

You slip inside the shack and carefully slide under the Oglemorooth's cot. Sandina and Luther start yelling, taunting the Oglemorooth to come get them. The Oglemorooth jumps off the cot in a surprised frenzy and stomps out the door. You reach up, grab the spoon from under the pillow, and take off. But as you come out the door you see the Oglemorooth turning back. He hasn't fallen for your trick. When he sees you run out the door, he turns around and comes after you.

Turn to page 61.

"Very well," replies Malgernopf. "Here, take your TV." He gives it to you and shoos you and Luther out of his room. You find yourselves in the cavern again, with no idea how to get out.

"Well," Luther says, "we might as well change the channel."

You switch the channel. On the screen appear several round shapes floating a few feet above the ground. You look up and see that the round shapes are actually creatures of some sort, with arms and legs sticking out of big, balloonlike bodies. They have propellers attached to their heads and they are floating through the air.

Turn to page 63.

Steering your bike to the left, along the lake shore, you turn onto a short path leading to the boathouse. To your surprise, Fingley keeps going around the lake. You decide not to worry about him.

You jump off your bike, grab the TV, and run to one of the pedal boats. You get into the boat and start pedaling out across the lake. On the other side of the lake you see some woods, with no road close by. Once you reach them, you should be able to take off and finally lose Fingley.

Having the lake all to yourself is really quite pleasant, you think, as you watch the ducks swim by. But your thoughts are interrupted by the roar of an engine coming from behind you. You turn around. It's Fingley, chasing you in a motorboat!

Your first reaction is just to give up. It seems you'll never escape. Then you consider your options more calmly. Perhaps you should meet Fingley head on and try to have it out with him once and for all. The only other thing you can think of, although it's risky, is to activate the anti-matter device and hope to return things to normal.

If you decide to meet Fingley head on,
turn to page 29.

If you turn the TV on and change the channel,
turn to page 93.

You smile at the agents as the TV sails over the railing. They stare in shock as it plunges into the water below.

The FBI takes you into custody, but eventually releases you. Back home with your parents, you tell them you're sorry you destroyed their invention.

"Well," your mother says philosophically, "in the end, the right place for the antimatter device may be the bottom of the ocean anyway."

The End

Soon the slurping noises stop and you hear a loud belch. There is movement in the shack, then the unmistakable sound of snoring.

"Let's go," you say.

Luther and Sandina follow you to the door. You open it slowly, slip into the shack, and tiptoe through the kitchen to a little back room where the Oglemorooth is snoring on his cot. Very quietly you move to the cot and slip your hand underneath the pillow. But the Oglemorooth's head is heavy. There is no way you can get your hand under there. Somehow you will have to get the Oglemorooth off his pillow so you can reach the spoon.

If you think you should look for some rope in order to tie up the Oglemorooth, turn to page 72.

If you decide to create a diversion in order to get the Oglemorooth off the cot, turn to page 55.

You race up the trail, but soon you realize that the Oglemorooth is faster than you and will catch you if you stay on the trail. Desperate, you plunge into the woods, hoping to lose him in the dense tangle of undergrowth.

You don't pay much attention to where you are going as you dodge bushes and branches and jump over fallen logs. Suddenly you find yourself at the edge of a precipice. Below is a deep gorge. The Oglemorooth is not far behind you.

Several vines hang from the trees at the edge of the gorge. Should you try to swing across on one of them? Or should you climb a tree and hope the Oglemorooth runs past you?

If you want to swing across on the vine, turn to page 16.

If you want to climb the tree, turn to page 44.

You turn the TV on and change the channel just as the FBI men converge on you. Immediately you are aware of bitter cold. There's nothing around you but ice and waste. The sun of whatever solar system you are in is just a small orange orb low in the sky. You have never felt anything like this cold. It penetrates your body incredibly quickly.

You reach for the channel switch with shaking fingers. You manage to get hold of it and try to turn it—but it is frozen. Your last thought, as your body temperature plummets, is that at least you have saved the antimatter device from the agents.

The End

You stand up and find that you feel very light. You take a step and go bounding into the air, then come slowly back to the ground. Luther tries it too and says, "I feel as light as a feather!"

"This planet must have very little gravity," you say.

"Low gravity indeed!" one of the passing balloon-people says. He stops and looks you over. He has a waxed black mustache, hair parted down the middle, and wears round spectacles. "I'll have you know this is one of the most serious planets in this universe. Why, we deal with the weightiest of matters!"

"Such as?" Luther prods.

"Harumph! Well, such as—such as—for instance . . ."

"Oh, don't listen to him," says another balloon-man as he floats by. This one has a long thin face and stiff black hair. "He doesn't know from beans."

If you ask the man with the mustache if he can help you, turn to page 77.

If you decide you want to get out of this world, turn to page 117.

The door swings open, and sitting in an easy chair, watching your TV, is the little man with pointed ears. He looks up as you enter.

"Very good!" Malgernopf says cordially. "You certainly outwitted the old Oglemorooth! Thoroughly enjoyable. Come in, please. Have a seat."

The little man's voice is so full of warmth that you forget your anger at him. Instead, you accept a cup of tea and eat a few ginger cookies.

"Now that you've entertained me," he says, "what can I do for you?"

"You can give me back my TV!" you say. "And you can tell me how to return to the world I came from."

Turn to page 73.

"Forget it," you tell the spider. "We don't have time for chasing Oglemorooths."

"Too bad," the spider says, crawling back up to the roof. "Don't say I didn't try to help you."

"Hey!" you call. "Come back. Who is that guy behind the stone door?"

You can barely hear the spider's voice. "You'll never get your TV back from old Malgernopf. He's far too clever."

You and Luther look at each other in dismay. Then you notice a little button set in the stone by the doorway. You push it. Slowly the stone door opens and the little man called Malgernopf is facing you.

"Well!" he says grumpily. "A fine pair of adventurers you are! I've been watching you on your TV, you know. Scared of the Oglemorooth, are you?"

"All I want is to get my TV back so I can return to my world."

Malgernopf gestures toward Luther. "And what about him?"

"I'm just along for the ride," Luther says.

Go on to the next page.

Malgernopf rubs his beard and grumbles to himself before saying, "You're obviously not going to provide me with any entertainment, so I'll make you an offer. I think I can get you back to the world you came from. But the price for that is the TV. If you leave the TV, I'll get you back. Otherwise, you can have the TV, and good-bye."

If you accept Malgernopf's offer,
turn to page 85.

If you say you want the TV back,
turn to page 57.

"I was asking if you might be able to help me," you say to the balloon-man. You point to the TV. "I've got this device which allows me to travel between worlds, but I don't know how to make it get me back to my own world, which is where I really want to be."

The balloon-man clears his throat. "Well, I've never seen one of those contraptions, but there is no doubt in my mind that with vigorous application of the scientific method we will solve your problem, and any other problems that come along."

"Great!" Luther says.

The balloon-man picks up the TV. "Now, how is it that you travel about with this thing?"

"You just turn the little dial on the right side," you say.

The man peers at the dial and says, "The solution is obvious! You merely apply the method of experimentation to this device, and once the laws of mathematical probability run their course, you will ultimately be taken back to your world."

"What?" Luther says.

"In layman's terms," the balloon-man explains, "you just keep switching the channel until you arrive at the place you want to be. It's bound to happen sooner or later!"

If you decide to follow the balloon-man's advice, turn to page 78.

If you're sure there must be some other way, turn to page 74.

You sit down in front of the control panel of the transporter. You realize that before you try to figure out how to navigate the thing, you have to find out where in the wide reaches of space you are traveling.

You look around. There's the ship's computer. Perhaps you should ask it about the planet Earth. You also see several storage lockers built into the walls. Perhaps you could find some star charts that would help you determine your location.

If you want to ask the computer about Earth, turn to page 96.

If you look for some star charts, turn to page 90.

"We'd better get the real spoon," you say to Luther. "After all, that's what we said we'd do."

Sandina says it's time to go down into the valley. The three of you descend into the thick forest on a narrow, winding trail. An ominous silence surrounds you.

The Oglemorooth's shack appears through the trees beside a swamp. You creep up to a window. Inside you see the Oglemorooth, an enormous troll-like creature with curly blond hair, blue eyes, and an upturned nose. He is spooning spider eggs from a bowl on to a piece of toast. His meal is accompanied by disgusting slurping noises.

"He's kind of pretty for an Oglemorooth," Luther comments.

"Pretty on the outside," Sandina says, "but nasty on the inside."

Sandina leads you away from the window. "He'll take his nap as soon as he's done eating," she whispers.

Turn to page 60.

You tiptoe back to the door where Luther and Sandina are waiting and say, "I need some rope to tie up the Oglemorooth."

Sandina gives you a skeptical look. "That's very risky," she says. "Where will we find rope? We'll have to use vines."

The three of you collect some good strong vines from the forest, then creep back into the Oglemorooth's shack. While Luther works on the feet, you carefully loop the vines around the Oglemorooth's arms and tie them to the bedpost. Luther gently lifts the Oglemorooth's head off the pillow and you reach underneath and grab the spoon.

The Oglemorooth starts to wake, so the three of you leave quickly. As you head up the path, you hear a piteous wail from inside the shack. You feel sorry for the Oglemorooth. Still, you're glad he's tied up so he can't come after you.

On the other side of the pass, Sandina prepares to lower you and Luther back down the well. You thank her for her help. She waves good-bye, saying, "I'm sure all the spiders around here will be grateful to you."

The orange spider glows with pleasure when you present the spoon. "It's easy to get in the stone door." he says. "Just ring that doorbell to the right of the door. The little man inside is named Malgernopf."

Sure enough, the button is right there. You press it.

Turn to page 64.

Malgernopf furrows his brow. "Hmm. I'm not sure exactly how to accomplish that. But," he says, taking his toolbox down from a shelf, "I'll have a look inside there and see what I can do."

Malgernopf takes the back off the TV and pokes around for a while. "I think I've got it," he announces. You come closer for a look. He is holding a wire in each hand. "When you touch these wires together, you should be transported back to the world from which this machine originated. At least, as far as I can tell."

You take the two wires in your fingers and say good-bye to Malgernopf, then to Luther. "I'll miss you."

"I'll miss you, too," Luther says. For the first time, he looks sad.

You move away from Malgernopf and Luther, then touch the wires together. Sparks fly and you are knocked backward. When you sit up, you are on the floor of your parents' lab, the open TV in front of you. You leave it right where it is and run to find your parents.

The End

"There must be some other way," you tell the balloon-man.

"Humph!" he replies. "So you don't believe in the scientific method."

"That's not true," Luther objects.

"Here," the balloon-man says, "take back your contraption. I want nothing more to do with it."

He begins to hand the TV back down to you from his floating position in the air, but it slips. You freeze for a moment, then recover your senses and dive for it. Luckily, you make the catch.

The TV is upside down when you catch it. You notice a button on the bottom marked RESET. "Look at this!" you say. "I'll bet that's how to get back to my world."

"But that's completely unscientific," the balloon-man says. "You have no idea what that button will do."

"That may be," you say, "but I'm going to try it."

You walk a few feet away. "This might be goodbye," you say to Luther.

"Good luck," Luther says.

You press the button. Suddenly you feel as if the ground is falling out from under you. It goes faster and faster, then everything blurs.

When you can see again, you are back in your parents' lab. Your parents look shocked at first, then blurt out, "How—?"

"It was easy," you say. "Science—and luck."

The End

You need more information. Looking over the file on Earth, you see two possibilities: You could find out about parallel worlds, or you could look up the Antimatter Society.

If you want information on parallel worlds, turn to page 80.

If you check up on the Antimatter Society, turn to page 84.

"Perhaps you can help me," you say to the balloon-man with the mustache. "I'm trying—"

"I wouldn't ask him for help," the long-faced man says. "He's nothing but a scientist. He's a charlatan, a fake."

"Oh, ho ho," the man with the mustache replies. "Look who's talking, you nincompoop."

The other man's face turns red and he bursts out, "Why you—" Suddenly he pulls out a pin, and before you can stop him, he punctures the man with the mustache, who deflates with a loud hiss into a limp pile of clothes on the ground.

"That'll teach you!" the other man says as he floats away, laughing.

"Please help me," the deflated man says. "I can't get up. My bones are made of lead, and unless you inflate me again I'll never be able to move from this spot!"

"How do we do that?" Luther asks.

"One of you must find a pump. The other one can reach in my pocket and get out my patch kit to repair the place where that nincompoop pricked me. Oh, my, this is the third time this month."

Luther runs off to get a pump while you patch up the man's punctured skin. Once you've pumped him up again, he pats his stomach and says, "Ah, that feels much better. Those nincompoops just can't get it through their thick heads that science is a serious endeavor. Now, what were you asking?"

Turn to page 68.

"We'll try it," you say to the balloon-man.

"You can't fail," he assures you. "It's the scientific method!"

"Science is great!" Luther exclaims. He turns to you and says, "Can I come?"

"Sure," you say. "I may need the company."

You get right down to business, methodically switching from channel to channel. There seem to be an endless number of worlds. You and Luther see many amazing things, but you go on and on without finding your world.

A year later, you arrive on yet another unfamiliar planet. You are completely exhausted. You and Luther slump down against the TV. Luther remarks, "This could go on forever."

"You're right," you say.

The End

You sit down for a moment and review your situation: You woke up this morning to find that everybody was gone. The Artificial Intelligence said the inhabitants of the planet had been removed, and that you weren't on Earth at all, but a planet called Mu. It said Earth was a fictitious planet in something called the Realm of Unreality.

It occurs to you that you may want to alter the transporter's current course. On the other hand, maybe you should send out a distress signal and hope a friendly ship will answer.

If you want to send a distress signal, turn to page 91.

If you decide to try to navigate the transporter yourself, turn to page 69.

80

Under the science heading, you ask for the file on parallel worlds. The computer directs you to RELIGION. There you find it:

PARALLEL WORLDS: A theory or belief held in pre-Imperial times. According to the theory, the universe is constantly dividing into alternative worlds. Many—perhaps an infinite number—of these parallel worlds exist side by side, simultaneously, without disrupting one another. The theory is believed to have originated with the Quantum Mystics. They claimed that by intense meditation they could gain knowledge of parallel worlds, and actually travel between these worlds.

After reading the file you realize there is only one thing for you to do.

Turn to page 10.

You decide to live the good life. Why worry about where everyone else is, you think, when you can satisfy your every material desire?

You settle down in the largest mansion you can find. It has a swimming pool, a tennis court, a croquet green, and a bowling alley. The horses are still in the stable and the Rolls Royces are in the garage. Every room in the mansion is your room.

Occasionally you make forays into the city to pick up supplies. You can have almost any kind of food, and you try everything. You listen to every record you've ever wanted, watch every movie on videocassette, and read every book on the shelves. You have no responsibilities. You don't have to work. If you don't feel like doing the dishes you can just throw them away.

One day, eating breakfast on the veranda, you look up from your plate and ask yourself: Are you happy with your life at the mansion? Or, if you are dissatisfied, do you want to travel?

If you want to stay at the mansion, turn to page 112.

If you want to leave, turn to page 92.

"Two plus two equals twenty-two," you say to the Artificial Intelligence.

"Incorrect, Muon," it responds. "Two plus two—"

"Truth is false," you interrupt. "Peace is war, up is down—"

"Error, error. Please rephrase your statement." The Artificial Intelligence sounds flustered. You pick up the pace, reciting:

"'Twas brillig, and the slithy toves
Did gyre and gimble in the wabe:
All mimsy were the borogoves . . ."

"Language unknown," says the Artificial Intelligence. "Danger. Danger."

You make up your own nonsense: "Incidental transformation employs capillary incense. Elephant tides ride side by side. Smile, snuffbox—"

"Circuit overload!" the Artificial Intelligence cries. It reaches for the WARNING button, but you knock its hand away. It spins around, its limbs flap wildly, sparks fly, and then it collapses on the floor. You are now in control of an interstellar transporter in hyperwarp overdrive in the depths of space!

Turn to page 79.

You ask the computer for the file on the Antimatter Society. After a few moments the file comes up:

ANTIMATTER SOCIETY: A secret society, which existed during the Anarchic Era, before the Rule of Empire. Its members, mostly renegade scientists and explorers, conducted experiments with exotic substances, including antimatter, which they believed to be the key to the universe. Combining ancient rituals and practices with scientific information, the society claimed to have unlocked secrets of the Ancient Era, including the location of the planet "Earth." After the establishment of the Rule of Empire, this subversive group was suppressed, and is now all but extinct.

The file gives you a glimmer of hope. Maybe you can find surviving members of the Antimatter Society. Surely they would be interested to meet an authentic Earthling, and in exchange, perhaps they could tell you how to get back.

Turn to page 111.

"All right, you can have the TV," you say to Malgernopf. "Just get me back to the world I came from. And get Luther back, too."

Malgernopf smiles and motions for you to follow him. He takes you down a steep stone staircase to a small, windowless room filled with more scientific and electrical equipment than you have ever seen. It is strewn about in no apparent order, but Malgernopf seems to know where to find what he wants. He seats you and Luther in chairs, connects a number of electrodes to you, and stands before a control panel.

"Ready?" he asks.

"Ready," you and Luther say together. Malgernopf throws some switches. You feel a jolt, then lose consciousness.

When you come to, you and Luther are lying on the ground. Your head is pounding.

The pounding is increased by a terrible roar that sounds as if it is right next to your ear. "Look!" Luther screams, pointing upward.

It's the giant lizard again! It's hovering right over you. Its greedy, bloodthirsty eyes are even more horrible than they were last time—because they are about to devour you.

"What's going on?" Luther screams.

All at once you realize what has happened. "We forgot to tell Malgernopf which worlds we originally came from!" you say. Seconds later the lizard has you in its jaws.

The End

86

With the help of the computer, you teach yourself how to navigate, and set course for the Realm of Unreality.

Your heart is pounding as the ship crosses the border. WARNING, the computer monitor tells you, ENTERING DANGER AREA.

You look around. The Realm of Unreality doesn't look much different from what you just left. But the transporter starts picking up speed, as if it is being drawn into a whirlpool.

WARNING, CRAFT APPROACHING MAXIMUM SPEED, the computer screen reads, then changes to WARNING, ANTIMATTER CLUSTER AHEAD. An enormous jolt knocks you to the floor as you are deflected away from the Antimatter Cluster.

Your speed continues to increase. DANGER! DANGER! DANGER! the computer screen flashes. The readings on the control panel go wild. They show nothing but -------, and the transporter is still accelerating. You are plastered against the wall, as if a giant hand is pressing you there. The last thing you see before you pass out is the computer screen, which shows only pulsating blips.

Turn to page 98.

When the Artificial Intelligence appears to be preoccupied with navigating the transporter, you steal up behind it. But, sensing your movement, it wheels around and stuns you with a photon beam from its finger.

When you come to, the transporter has landed and the Artificial Intelligence is pushing you out the hatch. You descend to the ground on a cushion of air. The transporter takes off, and you look around at the planet that may be your new home.

It is a desolate, barren place of makeshift shacks and crooked, dusty streets under a hot sun. You feel hopeless. If this is where everyone you know has been taken . . .

You walk down one of the streets and come to a little square in which someone is working a water pump. The person at the pump looks up. You stop, astounded. You feel as if you are looking into a mirror—the person looks exactly like you!

Turn to page 95.

The Artificial Intelligence keeps counting down the seconds—". . . four, three . . ."

You reach the car door just as the Artificial Intelligence says, "two, one." You put the key in the ignition. The Artificial Intelligence mechanically raises its finger and points it at you. A blinding photon beam issues from it and reduces you and your car to ashes.

The End

You rummage around until you finally dig up some dust-covered star charts in the bottom of one of the lockers. The Artificial Intelligence probably had no use for them.

You spread out the charts. It takes a long time to figure out how the various readings on the control panel of the transporter relate to the coordinates on the charts, but eventually you are able to plot your position.

A large blank space on the charts, not too far from your present position, attracts your attention. It is labeled REALM OF UNREALITY. A footnote says, "Travel not recommended in this area." Many points in the area on the map are marked with warnings such as ANTIMATTER CLUSTER, BLACK HOLE, DELUSION ZONE.

If Earth is fictitious, you think, perhaps the place to look for it is in the Realm of Unreality. On the other hand, it may be very dangerous. Nearby is a friendly sounding planet, Yuba CT. Maybe you should go there.

If you head for Yuba CT, turn to page 23.

If you want to set course for the Realm of Unreality, turn to page 86.

You look up the intergalactic distress signal and broadcast it over the transporter's radio. At first there's no response, but after a few hours you notice out of the porthole two silvery specks gaining on you. You wait and watch as they cover the vast distance of space separating you.

As the spaceships draw closer, you're not sure you like the look of them. The monitor on the transporter warns, TWO ARMED STARSHIPS APPROACHING. Then it asks, ACTIVATE AUTOMATIC DEFENSE SYSTEM?

You don't want to start a fight, especially if the starships can help you. But perhaps you should activate the defense system as a precaution.

If you activate the automatic defense system, turn to page 104.

If you wait for communication from the starships, turn to page 110.

You're dissatisfied with the quiet life at the mansion. You decide to set out and see the world—and perhaps also find other people.

First you go to the library and read all you can on how to fly an airplane. You figure it will be the best way to get around. Then, taking your pilot manuals with you, you go to the airport and spend several days practicing flying an airplane short distances. Finally, when you think you are ready, you load the plane with supplies and take off.

You fly all over the globe. You see amazing things—remote mountain ranges, endless deserts, teeming tropical forests, silent stretches of ice. But you never do run into any other people.

The End

Suddenly you are sitting in an easy chair in the living room of your house. Your parents are on the sofa, watching TV. On the screen, you see your adventures.

Your mother turns to you and says calmly, "That was very exciting. We're certainly glad you saved the antimatter device."

You hesitate before asking, "Am I really back in the *real* world?"

"What do you mean?" your father asks, puffing on his pipe.

"Well, how do I know this isn't just another parallel universe? This all seems pretty strange to *me*."

Your father wrinkles his brow and removes his pipe from his mouth. "I suppose you *don't* know."

"That's true," your mother says. "There could be any number of universes just like this one except for a few details. There's no way to tell."

From now on, you vow, you'll pay attention to the details of this world. Then perhaps you'll be able to tell whether you're really back.

The End

"Who are *you*?" you both ask, mouths gaping.

You approach each other warily. You can't help but feel somewhat outraged that someone else would dare to look just like you.

Finally you say, "What is this place?"

"Erid," your double replies. "The planet of exile. The Empire"—the word is said with unconcealed hatred—"has removed all Muons to this planet, which they call our 'homeland.' But it's only an excuse to exploit us in their uranium mines here. Aren't you a Muon? You look like one."

"I don't think so," you say.

"Unless . . ." Suddenly the double's eyes narrow with suspicion. "Unless you're an Artificial Intelligence sent here to deceive me."

You wonder if you should try to convince your double that you are not an Artificial Intelligence. Or should you just get out of there?

If you keep talking, turn to page 99.

If you get out fast, turn to page 107.

After you learn how to call up files from the transporter's computer, you go to the data banks on "Planets of Outlying Regions" and ask for the file on Earth.

It takes the computer a few seconds to locate the file. The information is displayed on the screen:

EARTH: A mythical planet invented by ancient tale-makers. This planet was supposed to exist in a "parallel world" (qv). In the tales, Earth was reputed to be the home of numerous strange and wonderful land forms, plants, and animals, as well as primitive but lovable beings known as humans. In the Anarchic Era, members of the Antimatter Society (qv) claimed to have discovered the planet Earth in a Delusion Zone in the Realm of Unreality. However, the claims have never been confirmed, and scientists are certain they are unprovable.

"But it's real!" you find yourself saying to the computer. "Earth is real!"

Then you feel doubtful. Maybe you've just been living in a Delusion Zone until now.

If you want to do some more research, turn to page 75.

If you decide you've been deluded and should forget about planet Earth, turn to page 118.

"I don't know about this," you say to Dr. Fingley. "It doesn't sound quite right to me."

You can see the anger in Fingley's eyes. He clenches his fists. "Listen," he says, "if you don't let me have that thing, we'll be stuck in this empty world forever."

"What are you going to do?" you ask, stalling for time.

Fingley doesn't answer. You can see that he is getting ready to spring for the TV. You must decide quickly—should you grab the TV and hope you can outrun him, or should you try to knock him down and then escape?

If you grab the TV, turn to page 15.

If you try to knock Fingley down as he springs, turn to page 18.

When you come to, all is calm. The readings on the control panel are back to normal. The only thing that is out of commission is the computer.

You glance out the port window, and your eyes open wide. Before you is the planet Saturn. You're back in your own solar system! You pass by Jupiter, then Mars. As you approach Earth, the communicator picks up a transmission that assures you that you've really returned to your home planet.

You decide to take another cruise around the solar system before landing on Earth. You imagine how amazed everyone will be when they see you land in the transporter, and how surprised they'll be to learn that they inhabit the Realm of Unreality.

The End

"I am *not* an Artificial Intelligence," you say firmly. "And why would I want to deceive you?"

Your double looks you over. "No, I guess you're too real-looking to be an Artificial Intelligence. A lot of people in the Empire want to deceive me. I'm an agent with the rebels who are fighting the Empire." Your double notices the look of surprise on your face and adds, "I know I'm a bit young to be an agent. But when you're fighting the Empire you grow up fast."

You decide to tell your double your story. When you're finished, the double thinks for a moment, then says, "It sounds like you're from a parallel world. I don't know how else to explain this."

You nod slowly. You've heard your parents talk about parallel worlds before in connection with their antimatter research, but you never could find out exactly what they meant.

You and your double are silent for a moment. Then you look at each other and burst out laughing at the strange situation. "Come on," your double says. "My parents are physicists. They may be able to help you get back to your world."

Turn to page 105.

"An antimatter device," Dr. Yuma explains, "ruptures the fabric of space and time, causing those near it to be transported to a parallel world."

"Does this mean you also have an antimatter device?" you ask.

"No, but on Mu we had developed one to use as a weapon in the rebellion against the Empire. But just before we were removed to Erid, it was stolen by a scientist working as a spy for the Empire—Dr. Fingley."

"Dr. Fingley!" you exclaim. "There's a Dr. Fingley in my parents' lab too."

"Interesting that the names should be the same," Dr. Yuma says.

"We're trying to make another antimatter device," Dr. Xerba says. "The problem is that we don't have all the material we need here to do it. We salvaged some things from our lab, but we still lack many items."

"Wait a minute," you say. "Wouldn't it make sense that if Fingley stole the device in your world, he may also have stolen it in mine, and that somehow I got transported to Mu along with him? Which would mean . . ."

"Fingley may still be on Mu with the antimatter device!" Pollux breaks in.

The scientists' eyes light up. "Yes," Dr. Yuma says. "Of course, there's no guarantee it happened as you said, or that he's still there. But it's worth a try."

Go on to the next page.

"A new antimatter device would be invaluable," Dr. Xerba adds.

"But how do we get it?" you ask.

"We'll go there," Pollux says. "We're making contact with the underground in the next day or so. We'll set up a secret rendezvous with a rebel cruiser. It will take us back to Mu, and we will see what we find."

Turn to page 106.

You continue to drive around the city, watching for signs of life. It's fun to be able to drive anywhere you want on the empty streets, but at the same time you doubt you'd want to be without other people for very long.

As these thoughts go through your mind, you stop paying attention to where you're going. You find yourself in a part of town you don't recognize. All around you are broken-down warehouses, loading docks, and vacant lots. You are lost.

A strange object sitting in an empty space near an old cement factory attracts your attention. It is an odd-shaped white thing about the size of your bedroom, perched ten feet off the ground on spindly metal legs. You stop the car and get out to take a closer look.

As you approach the thing you hear a whooshing sound. What appears to be a man floats down from the object, as if riding a cushion of air. You stop and stare at him as he walks toward you with jerky movements.

"What are you doing here, Muon?" he asks in a metallic, evenly measured voice. You take a closer look at him. His eyes are glassy and his skin does not look real. You realize that he is not a human being but a robot dressed up to look human.

"Muon?" you ask.

"No, I am not a Muon. You are a Muon," the metallic voice answers. "Muon: an inhabitant of the planet Mu. You have ten seconds to answer the question or I will terminate you. Ten, nine, eight—"

Turn to page 109.

AUTOMATIC DEFENSE SYSTEM ACTIVATED, the monitor says. Seconds later a voice comes over the communicator: "This is Captain Smerk of the Imperial Patrol. Distress signal received. We have identified you as Imperial Transport number 472, under the control of Artificial Intelligence unit number 984651A. State the nature of your problem."

You nervously reply, "I, uh, changed my mind. Everything's all right."

There is silence, followed by: "Prepare to be boarded."

A pod emerges from one of the starships. The computer flashes red, REPEL BOARDING ATTEMPT, and a streak of white annihilates the pod. There's a rapid exchange of beams between your ship and the starships—then the starships explode in a spectacular burst of white. Meanwhile, legends have been flashing across the computer screen: DEFLECT BEAM and EVASIVE MANEUVER and COUNTERATTACK.

Now the screen reads simply, ATTACK REPELLED. MINOR DAMAGE. AUTOMATIC DEFENSE SYSTEM DEACTIVATED. But a few seconds later, it tells you, CRUISERS APPROACHING, and again asks, ACTIVATE AUTOMATIC DEFENSE SYSTEM?

Before you answer, a voice comes over the communicator: "This is Rebel Cruiser. Good show! Who's in there, anyway?"

"It's just me," you reply. "Please take this thing off my hands."

Turn to page 116.

You are not suprised to find that your double's parents look just like yours. They are introduced as Drs. Xerba and Yuma. You tell them your name. Your double adds, "And my name is Pollux."

You tell your story again, and ask the physicists if there is any way they can help you get back to your world.

"Possibly," Dr. Xerba says. "Presumably, since you're from a parallel world, your parents were working on an antimatter device?"

"I know they were involved in antimatter research," you reply. "What's an antimatter device?"

Turn to page 100.

In a few days you are on your way back to Mu. Soon you touch down in the empty neighborhood that looks exactly like your neighborhood at home.

You and Pollux carefully slip into the lab building at the university. Pollux is carrying a wafer-thin television set. You find Fingley's lab and stop at the door to listen. You can hear Fingley muttering to himself.

"He's here!" Pollux whispers. "Have you got the plan straight?"

You nod. Pollux disappears down the hall. You burst into Fingley's lab. Fingley practically jumps out of his skin as you stride into the room.

"Oh, it's only you," he says, his fingers trembling as he wipes his forehead.

You just smile, pick up the TV set, which is exactly like the one Pollux has, and dash out of the room.

Instead of running down the hall, you hide in a closet next door. Once Fingley recovers his wits, he runs after you. You hear him come out of his lab, then you hear Pollux cry from down the hall, "Come and get me, Fingley!"

Turn to page 114.

You back away from your double, then turn and dash down one of the streets.

You look behind to see your double chasing you, calling, "Hey! Come back!" But you keep running. After a while you lose the double in the maze of dusty streets.

You decide to keep moving in order to get as far away as you can. The ramshackle city seems to go on forever. You feel better as you put more and more distance between yourself and the square with the water pump.

But your relief doesn't last long. You discover that life on Erid is bleak. The only way to earn a living is to work in the Empire's uranium mines. The Imperial bosses for whom you work believe Muons are an inferior species and treat them like cattle. You have little to look forward to but an unhappy life in the mines or an early death from radiation sickness.

The End

108

You find the spare set of keys, go out to the garage, and start up the car. As you back down the driveway and turn onto the street, you feel a small tingle of excitement. It's the first time you've driven a car in the city. You realize that if it's true that you are the only one left in the world, you can go wherever you want and do whatever you want.

Driving through the empty streets, you see no one. Occasionally you spot a dog or cat crossing the street, but no people. However, stores, offices, and houses are still here, their doors open. It occurs to you that you have all the material goods of civilization at your disposal, as if they were made just for you. You find yourself wondering if you should just enjoy all of these things and live the good life while you can. Maybe the world is your oyster.

If you decide the world is your oyster, turn to page 81.

If you decide to look around some more with the hope of finding people, turn to page 102.

"I don't know what I'm doing here," you say quickly. "I just woke up and everyone was gone."

"Imperial order number 38476 dictates that all inhabitants of the planet Mu are to be removed," the robot says. "Please comply."

"But this is the planet Earth. Aren't you making a mistake?"

"The mistake is yours, Muon. 'Earth' is a fictitious planet in the Realm of Unreality. You, however, are an inhabitant of the planet Mu, located in the outer fringe of the Fourth Quadrant of the Great Empire. As a subject of the Empire you must obey the Leaders. Please board the interstellar transporter for removal. You have ten seconds to comply, or I will terminate you. Ten, nine, eight, seven—"

"Please don't!" you exclaim.

"I am an Artificial Intelligence," the imitation human says. "Do not try to appeal to my emotions. I do not have any. Seven seconds to termination. Six, five . . ."

If you decide to board the interstellar transporter, turn to page 115.

If you make a dash for your car, turn to page 88.

The starships continue to approach and the captain of one of them speaks to you over the communicator: "This is Captain Smerk of the Imperial Patrol. Distress signal received. We have identified you as Imperial Transport number 472, under the control of Artificial Intelligence unit #984651A. Prepare to be boarded."

You wait nervously as a pod is sent out from the starship. You open the air lock and let in an Imperial officer. He takes one look at you, at the inoperative Artificial Intelligence on the floor, and knocks you out with a blast from his particle weapon.

When you come to, you are in a prison cell on the starship. The captain enters and says sharply, "What were you doing on the transporter?"

"I was just trying to get back to planet Earth," you say.

He laughs mockingly. "So you're one of those lunatics who believe in planet 'Earth,' eh? Well, I suppose it doesn't matter. The Imperial Judge will find you either insane or guilty of stealing an interstellar transporter. Either way, the penalty is death."

The End

Once you figure out how to navigate the transporter, you begin your search. Taking care to avoid areas controlled by the Empire, you ask everyone you can find how to reach the Antimatter Society. Many tell you it has died out, but others say it has gone underground and is very secret. None have had direct contact with the Antimatter Society, but every time you are directed to someone who might know, they have a name of someone else who might know. You're confident that if you follow the trail long enough, you'll find your way back.

The End

Life at the mansion suits you fine. You have everything you could want. Nothing unpleasant gets in the way.

As your life goes on, your tastes become simpler and simpler. You visit the empty shell of civilization below less and less often. In your later days, you end up spending all your time by the pool, eating frozen pizzas, drinking root beer, and reading old Pogo books.

The End

Fingley runs after Pollux, and you quietly slip out of the closet once they have gone. You return to the cruiser with the TV. Pollux shows up a few minutes later, laughing. "Well, Fingley got his TV back from me all right. But he'll be disappointed when he finds out it's only a regular television set."

"Why does the antimatter device look like a TV, anyway?" you ask.

"Disguise," Pollux says simply. "Speaking of which—it's too bad we're losing you. You'd make a great 'double' agent. But now that we have the antimatter device, I can get you back to your world, and then take the device back to Erid."

The End

You quickly move to the interstellar transporter as the Artificial Intelligence continues counting down. Something opens above you and you are sucked up into the spaceship with a whoosh of air. The Artificial Intelligence joins you after a moment, and the doors of the transporter close.

The Artificial Intelligence sets the controls of the transporter. As it accelerates into hyperwarp overdrive, you think that surely with your real intelligence you will be able to outwit this Artificial Intelligence and get back home. But how? Perhaps you could could use illogic and nonsense to confuse it. On the other hand, maybe there is some way you can sneak up behind it and turn it off.

If you start speaking nonsense to the Artificial Intelligence, turn to page 82.

If you look for a chance to sneak up on it, turn to page 87.

A pod leaves the cruiser and soon you are joined in the transporter by two rebels. They slap you on the back and congratulate you on your victory over the Imperial starships.

"We'll take you back to our planetary outpost. You'll get a hero's welcome. You've captured a transporter and we'll be able to learn a lot from it. We'll overthrow this corrupt empire yet!"

You decide it's not such a bad thing to be doing, at least until you can figure out how to get back to Earth.

The End

"This place is crazy," you say to Luther. "Let's get out of here."

You and Luther step to the side as the two balloon-men continue their bickering. You switch the channel.

Unfortunately, the planet to which you are transported has no atmosphere and is very close to its sun. You and Luther are vaporized within seconds.

The End

You tell yourself that your life on Earth was only a delusion. What else would you expect, living in a Delusion Zone?

You manage to get the transporter to a nearby planet, and eventually you fall in with a group of the rebels trying to overthrow the Empire. They are impressed with your capture of the interstellar transporter. You join them and soon become an intergalactic pilot.

Every once in a while, in late night conversations, people will mention Earth and wonder if it doesn't really exist. You laugh and tell them that it's a delusive phase and that they'll get over it.

The End

ABOUT THE AUTHOR

JAY LEIBOLD was born in Denver, Colorado, and now lives in San Francisco, California. He has also written *Sabotage, Grand Canyon Odyssey,* and *Spy for George Washington* for the Choose Your Own Adventure series.

ABOUT THE ILLUSTRATOR

FRANK BOLLE studied at Pratt Institute. He has worked as an illustrator for many national magazines and now creates and draws cartoons for magazines as well. He has also worked in advertising and children's educational materials and has drawn and collaborated on several newspaper comic strips, including *Annie.* A native of Brooklyn Heights, New York, Mr. Bolle now works and lives in Westport, Connecticut.